To my team:
Fran, Laurie, Susan, Cassie, Jay,
Sam, Jimmy B., Cory, and Boris (who never
says I do a good job!).
A. H.

For the "Outlaws"—
Tracie, Caroline, and Mark.
J. B.

First edition 2002

Library of Congress Cataloging-in-Publication Data
Hest, Amy.
Make the team, Baby Duck! / by Amy Hest ; illustrated by Jill Barton.
p.   cm.
Summary: When Baby Duck is not sure she is ready to get
into the pool with the swim team, her grandfather encourages her.
ISBN 0-7636-1541-2
[1. Self-confidence—Fiction. 2. Swimming—Fiction.
3. Ducks—Fiction. 4. Grandfathers—Fiction.]
I. Barton, Jill, ill. II. Title.
PZ7.H4375 Mak 2002
[E]—dc21   2001058261

2 4 6 8 10 9 7 5 3 1

Printed in China

This book was typeset in OPTI Lucius Ad Bold.
The illustrations were done in pencil and watercolor.

Candlewick Press
2067 Massachusetts Avenue
Cambridge, Massachusetts 02140

visit us at www.candlewick.com

Make the Team, Baby Duck!

Amy Hest

illustrated by **Jill Barton**

CANDLEWICK PRESS
CAMBRIDGE, MASSACHUSETTS

It was the first day of summer. Baby Duck sat all by herself at the edge of the town pool. From time to time, she dipped her feet.

The water was very cold.

"Come on in, Baby!" called Mr. and Mrs. Duck.

"No," Baby said.

"But you love to swim!" Mr. and Mrs. Duck pranced in the pool. They danced in the pool and splashed. "Don't you remember what fun you had last summer?"

"No," Baby said.

"Look at this, Baby!"

Mr. Duck swam across the pool.

(He was a good swimmer.)

When he got to the other side, he waved.
Baby Duck did not wave back. She watched
the puffy clouds and the ruffles on her
swimsuit. She watched her little sister,
Hot Stuff, twirling in the pool.

"Look at us, Baby. We're nice and cool!"
Mrs. Duck bobbed and bounced in the water
with Hot Stuff. (They were good bobbers and
very good bouncers.) "Be a big girl now,
and jump right in!"

Baby did not jump.

Suddenly, the swim team marched across the grass.

"Look who's here!" clucked Mr. Duck.

"Oh, the lovely team!" trilled Mrs. Duck.

The swim team marched to the side of the pool and lined up their toes at the edge.

The coach blew his shiny silver whistle—
Tweeet! Tweeet!—and the whole team
jumped in the water, squealing.
Baby Duck shivered in the
summer sun, and sighed.

If only *she* could make the team.

"Hello, hello! I made the team!" Davy Duck came paddling by, paddling and pulling in the water.

"Me, too! Yaaaa for me!" Dotty Duck came gliding by, gliding and sliding in the water.

Baby Duck sang a little song.

"I wish I could make the team,
But I'm a slowly swimmer.
My arms get tired. . . .
What if I swallow water?"

Just then, Grampa came bounding across the grass.

"I was hoping you'd be here," he said, kissing her cheek.

He spread his towel right up close to Baby Duck.
"And I was hoping we could sit awhile on my
new towel. Like it?"

"Oh, yes," Baby said.

"Good," Grampa said.

"And *I* like how you
make wrinkles in the water,
and beautiful flutters. Is that very hard to do?"

"Oh, yes," Baby said.

"To make ripples like that,"
Grampa noted, "one needs
a pair of fine, strong feet."
Baby smiled at her
fine, strong feet.

The coach blew his shiny silver whistle—

Tweet! Tweet!—

and the swim team made

a circle in the water.

Bobble bobble, float! Bobble bobble, float!

"Looks like fun," Grampa said.

"Don't you think so, Baby?"

"Oh, yes," Baby said.

Baby Duck and Grampa sat watching the team.

From time to time, Baby sighed.

"Perhaps when you're ready, you'll be on the team. Would you like that?" Grampa asked.

"Oh, yes," Baby said. "But sometimes my arms are tired. It makes me slow."

"It happens," Grampa said. "From time to time, even champions slow down."

"And sometimes I swallow water. It makes me cough."

"It happens," Grampa said. "From time to time, even champions have to cough."

Baby Duck wriggled her toes over the water.

She kicked her fine, strong feet,

watching the team until she was ready.

And when she was ready, Baby Duck stood up and lined up her toes at the edge of the pool.

She waved to Mr. and Mrs. Duck and Hot Stuff.
After that, she squeezed her eyes tight and
jumped into the water.

She swam across the pool with her team, kicking very hard. Baby Duck swam and swam, and her arms did not get tired! She swam and swam, and she did not swallow water!

Afterward, she climbed out of
the pool and sang a new song.

"Swim swim swim,

I like and love my Grampa.

We have a pretty towel. . . .

Make the team, Baby Duck!"